AF166957

Anonymous

Catalogue of the Trustees, Faculty, and Students of the University of North Carolina, 1857-58

SALZWASSER VERLAG

Anonymous

Catalogue of the Trustees, Faculty, and Students of the University of North Carolina, 1857-58

Reprint of the original.

1st Edition 2023 | ISBN: 978-3-37514-576-7

Verlag (Publisher): Salzwasser Verlag GmbH, Zeilweg 44, 60439 Frankfurt, Deutschland
Vertretungsberechtigt (Authorized to represent): E. Roepke, Zeilweg 44, 60439 Frankfurt, Deutschland
Druck (Print): Books on Demand GmbH, In de Tarpen 42, 22848 Norderstedt, Deutschland

CATALOGUE

OF THE

TRUSTEES, FACULTY, AND STUDENTS

OF THE

UNIVERSITY OF NORTH CAROLINA,

1857—'58.

CHAPEL HILL:
PRINTED AT THE GAZETTE OFFICE.
....
1858.

3

CONTENTS.

———

TRUSTEES.

HIS EXCELLENCY THOMAS BRAGG,

Governor of the State of North Carolina, and ex-officio *President of the Board of Trustees.*

HON. CHARLES MANLY,

Secretary of the Board of Trustees.

NAME.	RESIDENCE.	APPOINTED.
John D. Hawkins, Esq.,	*Franklin Co.,*	1807.
Hon. Frederick Nash, LL. D.,	*Hillsborough,*	1807.
James C. Johnston, Esq.,	*Edenton,*	1818.
Hon. Willie P. Mangum, LL. D.,	*Orange Co.,*	1818.
Hon. Romulus M. Saunders,	*Raleigh,*	1819.
Solomon Graves, Esq.,	*Surry Co.*	1821.
Hon. John H. Bryan,	*Raleigh,*	1823.
Gen. William A. Blount,	*Washington,*	1825.
Hon. John R. Donnell,	*New Berne,*	1826.
Hon. Charles Manly,	*Raleigh,*	1820.
Hon. John L. Bailey,	*Hillsborough,*	1828.
Hon. John M. Morehead,	*Greensborough,*	1828.
Hugh Waddell, Esq.,	*Pittsborough,*	1828.
Hon. David L. Swain, LL. D.,	*Chapel Hill,*	1831.
Hon. Daniel M. Barringer,	*Charlotte,*	1832.
Charles L. Hinton, Esq.,	*Raleigh,*	1832.
Hon. William H. Battle, LL. D.,	*Chapel Hill,*	1833.
Hon. John R. J. Daniel,	*Halifax,*	1833.
Hon. William A. Graham, LL. D.,	*Hillsborough,*	1835.
Frederick J. Hill, M. D.,	*Brunswick Co.,*	1835.
Hon. Matthias E. Manly,	*New Berne,*	1835.
Gen. Samuel F. Patterson,	*Caldwell Co.,*	1835.

NAME.	RESIDENCE.	APPOINTED.
George F. Davidson, Esq.,	*Iredell Co.,*	1838.
William Eaton, Jr., Esq.,	*Warren Co.,*	1838.
Robert B. Gilliam, Esq.,	*Oxford,*	1838.
Hon. James T. Morehead,	*Greensborough,*	1838.
Burgess S. Gaither, Esq.,	*Morganton,*	1840.
George C. Mendenhall, Esq.,	*Jamestown,*	1840.
Bartholomew F. Moore, Esq.,	*Raleigh,*	1840.
John C. Williams, Esq.,	*Cumberland Co.,*	1840.
Patrick H. Winston, Esq.,	*Raleigh, .*	1840.
Jonathan Worth, Esq.,	*Asheborough,*	1840.
Thomas S, Ashe, Esq.,	*Wadesborough,*	1842.
Hon. John M. Dick,	*Greensborough,*	1842.
Hon. Thomas Ruffin, LL. D.,	*Alamance Co.,*	1842.
Calvin Graves, Esq.,	*Caswell Co.,*	1844.
Hon. William H. Washington,	*New Berne,*	1844.
Nicholas L. Williams, Esq.,	*Yadkin Co.,*	1844.
Daniel W. Courts, Esq.,	*Raleigh,*	1846.
John A. Gilmer, Esq.,	*Greensborough,*	1846.
Hon. John Kerr,	*Yanceyville,*	1846.
Walter F. Leak, Esq.,	*Richmond Co.,*	1846.
Giles Mebane, Esq.,	*Alamance Co.,*	1846.
Rev. Cushing B. Hassell,	*Williamston,*	1848.
Lewis Thompson, Esq.,	*Bertie Co.,*	1848.
William W, Avery, Esq.,	*Morganton,*	1850.
Hon. David S. Reid,	*Rockingham Co.,*	1850.
Samuel P. Hill, Esq.,	*Caswell Co.,*	1852.
Walter L. Steele, Esq.,	*Richmond Co.,*	1852.
John W. Cunningham, Esq.,	*Person Co.,*	1854.
Richard Dillard, M. D.,	*Chowan Co.,*	1856.
James F. Hardy, M. D.,	*Asheville,*	1856.
William W. Holden, Esq.,	*Raleigh,*	1856.
Thomas Settle, Esq.,	*Rockingham Co.,*	1856.

EXECUTIVE COMMITTEE.

HIS EXCELLENCY GOVERNOR BRAGG, *Chairman.*

HON. JOHN H. BRYAN,

DANIEL W. COURTS, ESQ.

MAJ. CHARLES L. HINTON,

HON. CHARLES MANLY,

BARTHOLOMEW F. MOORE, ESQ.,

HON. ROMULUS M. SAUNDERS.

BOARD OF EXAMINERS FOR 1858.

HON. JOHN L. BAILEY,

HON. DANIEL M. BARRINGER,

HON. WILLIAM H. BATTLE,

SAMUEL P. HILL, ESQ.,

WALTER F. LEAK, ESQ.

MISCELLANEOUS NOTICES.

THE ANNUAL COMMENCEMENT

IS ON THE FIRST THURSDAY IN JUNE.

THE COLLEGIATE YEAR

Is divided into two terms : the one commencing six weeks after the
first Thursday in June : the other six weeks after the Friday
succeeding the fourth Friday in November.

FACULTY.

HON. DAVID L. SWAIN, LL.D.,
PRESIDENT.

REV. JAMES PHILLIPS, D.D.,
Professor of Mathematics and Natural Philosophy.

MANUEL FETTER, A.M.,
Professor of the Greek Language and Literature.

HON. WILLIAM H. BATTLE, LL.D.,
Professor of Law.

REV. FORDYCE M. HUBBARD, A.M.,
Professor of the Latin Language and Literature.

REV. JOHN T. WHEAT, D.D.
Professor of Logic and Rhetoric.

REV. ALBERT M. SHIPP, A.M.,
Professor of History.

CHARLES PHILLIPS, A.M.,
Professor of Civil Engineering.

HILDRETH H. SMITH, A.M.
Professor of Modern Languages.

JOHN KIMBERLY, A.M.
Professor of Chemistry applied to Agriculture and the Arts.

WILLIAM J. MARTIN,
Professor of Chemistry, Mineralogy, and Geology.

SOLOMON POOL, A.M.,
Tutor of Mathematics.

JOSEPH B. LUCAS, A.M.,
Tutor of the Latin Language.

RICHARD H. BATTLE, Jr.,A.M.
Tutor of the Greek Language.

PETER E. SPRUILL, A.B.,
Tutor of the Latin Language.

SAMUEL S. JACKSON, A.M.,
Tutor of the Greek Language.

THADDEUS C. COLEMAN,
Tutor of Mathematics.

CHARLES A. MITCHELL, A.B.,
Tutor of Chemistry.

JOHN W. GRAHAM, A.B.,
Tutor of Mathematics.

WILLIAM L. ALEXANDER, A.B.,
Tutor of the Latin Language.

SOLOMON POOL, A.M.
Secretary of the Faculty.

UNDER-GRADUATES.

SENIOR CLASS.

NAME.	RESIDENCE.	ROOM.
Adams, William	Greensborough,	Mr. Craig's.
Allen, Edward L.	Fayetteville, Tenn.,	21, W. B.
Anderson, Robert W.	New Hanover Co.,	Mr. Hunt's.
Baker, James S.	Jackson Co., Fla.,	5, S. B.
Barnes, Jesse S.	Wilson Co.,	Mr. Scott's.
Bell, Edward S.	Bladen Springs, Ala.,	Mr. Jellee's.
Benbury, Lemuel C.	Edenton,	President Swain's.
Bitting, John H.	Germanton,	Mrs. Ashe's.
Bonner, William Jr.	Fayetteville, Tenn.,	Mr. Howell's.
Brinson, Samuel M.,	New Berne,	26, S. B.
Brown, Hugh T.	Wilkesborough,	Prof. Smith's.
Brown, Joseph A. C.	Davidson Co.,	Dr. Davis'
Bruce, Wilkins	Halifax Co., Va.,	Miss Hillyard's.
Buchanan, John B.	Richmond Co.,	Mrs. Snipes'.
Clark, Nevin D. J.	Montgomery Co.,	Mr. Weaver's.
Clement, Samuel W.	Granville Co.,	Mr Weaver's.
Coleman, William M.	Concord,	Prof. Smith's.
Cowan, Thomas	Wilmington,	20, S. B.
Cox, Cader G.	Onslow Co.,	Mr. Barbee's.
Davie, Ambrose Jr.	Montgomery Co., Tenn.,	Miss. Hillyard's.
Dowd, William C.	Wake Co.,	Mr. Mickle's.
Dugger, Macon T.	Warrenton,	Mrs. Mason's.
Faison, Peter B.	La Grange, Tenn.,	21, W. B.
Foreman, William G.	Pitt Co.,	4, S. B.
Gibson, John P.	Concord,	Mr. Marcom's.

NAME.	RESIDENCE.	ROOM.
Gibson, William H.	*Concord,*	Mr. Marcom's.
Gilmer, John A. Jr.	*Greensborough,*	Mr. Craig's.
Goodloe, David S. Jr. '	*Madison Co., Mi.,*	Mrs. Ashe's.
Goodloe, Winter H.	*Madison Co., Mi.*	Mrs. Ashe's
Goodman, John C.	*Gates Co.,*	Mr. Scott's.
Goza, S. Dupuy	*Carroll Par., La.,*	Prof. Wheat's.
Groover, James I.	*Thomas Co., Ga.,*	Mr. Hogan's.
Hadly, Oscar F.	*Sumter Co., Ala.,*	Miss Mallett's.
Hammond, William M.	*Wadesborough,*	Mr. Mickle's.
Harris, Robert T.	*McKinley, Ala.,*	Mr. Hudson's.
Harris, Thomas B.	*Warrenton, Ala.*	Mr. Hudson's.
Harvey, Addison	*Canton, Mi.,*	Mr. Marcom's.
Hay, Philip T.	*Rockingham Co.,*	Mrs. Ashe's.
Hill, James S.	*Stokes Co.,* *	Mrs. Ashe's.
Hilliard, Louis	*Nash Co.,*	Miss Mallett's.
Humphries, William W. Jr.	*Columbus, Mi.,*	Mr. Marcom's.
Hunt, James D.	*Izard Co., Ark.,*	Mr. Mickle's.
Isler, Stephen W.	*Goldsborough,*	Mr. Tilley's.
Johnson, Francis M.	*Davie Co.,*	Mrs. Ashe's.
Johnston, Robert D.	*Lincoln Co.,*	Mr. Marcom's.
Johnston, Zebulon M.	*Cabarrus Co.,*	Mr. Marcom's.
Jones, Hamilton C. Jr.	*Rowan Co.,*	Mrs. Ashe's.
Kerr, William L.	*Alamance Co.,*	Mr. Weaver's.
Little, William	*Raleigh,*	23, S. B.
Lord, William C.	*Salisbury,*	31, S. B.
Lusher, Nathaniel P.	*Memphis, Tenn.*	Mr. Loader's.
Macartney, Thomas N.	*Mobile, Ala.,*	Mr. Hudson's.
Mann, Rufus B.	*Granville Co.,*	Mr. Marcom's.
Marsh, James A.	*Asheborough,*	Dr. Davis'.
Marsh, Robert H.	*Chatham Co.,*	5, W. B.
Mason, Thomas W.	*Brunswick Co., Va.,*	President Swain's.
McAfee, LeRoy M.	*Shelby,*	Mrs. Hargrave's.
McAlister, Alexander C.	*Randolph Co.,*	Dr. Davis'.
McConnaughey, Joseph L.	*Rowan Co.,*	Mr. Carr's.
Miller, James A.	*Rutherfordton,*	Mr. Craig's.
Morehead, James T. Jr.	*Greensborough,*	25, S. B.

NAME.	RESIDENCE.	ROOM.
Murphy, William	*Salisbury,*	Mr. Craig's.
Perry, John M.	*Beaufort,*	Mr. Mickle's.
Philips, Frederick	*Edgecombe Co.,*	Mr. Marcom's.
Richmond, John M.	*Fairfield Dist., S. C.,*	22, S. B.
Ringo, Joseph II.	*Fayetteville, Tenn.,*	15, W. B.
Scales, James T.	*Henry Co., Va.,*	25, S. B.
Singeltary, Richard W.	*Pitt Co.*	15, S. B.
Smith, Benjamin G.	*Halifax Co.,*	5, S. B.
Stewart, Daniel	*Richmond Co.,*	Mrs. Snipes'.
Sutton, William T. Jr.	*Bertie Co.,*	Mrs. Lewis'.
Swain, Richard C.	*Chapel Hill,*	President Swain's.
Swayze, Caldwell C.	*Opelousas, La.,*	23, S. B.
Sykes, Edward T.	*Columbus, Mi.,*	Mr. Hudson's.
Sykes, S. Turner	*Columbus, Mi.,*	Mr. Hudson's.
Tate, Henry H.	*Gaston Co.,*	14, S. B.
Tate, John W.	*Gaston Co.,*	14, S. B.
Tatum, John D.	*Milledgeville, Ga.,*	Mr. Phillips'.
Twitty, William L.	*Rutherford Co.,*	Mrs. Hargrave's.
Wade, Thomas B.	*Williamson Co., Tenn.,*	Mrs. Kirkland's.
Walker, James A.	*Wilmington,*	20, S. B.
Washington, Augustine B.	*Memphis, Tenn.,*	Mrs. Ashe's.
Watlington, James S.	*Caswell Co.,*	Mrs Hargrave's.
Westray, Samuel E,	*Nash Co.,*	Mrs. Williams'.
Whitaker, William	*Davenport, Iowa,*	23, E. B.
White, Joseph M.	*Marianna, Fla.,*	22, S. B.
Whitehead, Willie W.	*Kenansville,*	Mr. Barbee's.
Whitfield, Boaz	*Demopolis, Ala.,*	Mr. Hudson's.
Whitted, Thomas S.	*Bladen Co.,*	Mr. Watson's.
Williams, Joseph	*Yadkin Co.,*	Mr. Craig's.
Williamson, John W.	*Caswell Co.,*	Prof. Smith's.
Wright, Julius W.	*Wilmington,*	Dr. Moore's.
Young, David J.	*Granville Co.,*	Mr. Nunn's.
Young, William H.	*Granville Co.,*	Mr. Nunn's.

JUNIOR CLASS.

NAME.	RESIDENCE.	ROOM.
Bacot, Peter B.	Darlington Dist., S. C.	21, S. B.
Badger, Richard C.	Raleigh,	18, E. B.
Badgett, Thomas J.	Caswell, Co.,	10, W. B.
Ballard, John W.	Wake Co.,	Mr. Loader's.
Barnes, George B.	Northampton Co.,	20, E. B.
Beasley, James E.	Plymouth,	Mr. Watson's.
Bein, Hugh II.	New Orleans, La.,	Mr. Jollee's.
Bonner, Thomas P.	Bath,	Mrs. Williams'.
Boyce, Jesse T.	Clarksville, Texas,	Mrs. Morrow's
Boylan, John S.	Raleigh,	32, S. B.
Bustin, James G.	Halifax Co.,	23, E. B.
Calloway, Abner S.	Wilkesborough,	Mrs. Hargrave's.
Campbell, James G. Jr.	Opelousas, La.,	Mrs. Lewis'.
Cates, Rutilius P.	Shreveport, La.,	Mr. Guthrie's.
Coffin, James P.	Knoxville, Tenn.,	Mrs. Hargrave's.
Cole, John W.	Richmond Co.,	Mrs. Ashe's.
Cole, Robert W.	Greensborough,	18, W. B.
Cook, John T.	Warrenton,	Mrs. Mason's.
Costin, Andrew J.	Wilmington,	Mrs. Williams'.
Cozart, William M. Jr.	Columbus, Mi.,	Mr. Loader's.
Croom, C. Stephens	New York City,	Mr. Nunn's.
Daniel, Henry R.	Bladen Co.,	Mr. Waitt's
Davis, Edward H.	Pasquotank Co.,	Mr. Hunt's.
Dixon, George F.	Alamance Co.,	Mr. Weaver's.
Duncan, John Jr.	Matagorda Co., Texas,	Dr. Mallett's.
Eure, Mills L.	Gates Co.,	12, E. B.
Evans, Thomas C.	Milton,	Mr. Guthrie's.
Ferguson, Isaac R.	Randolph Co., Ga.,	18, E. B.
Fetter, Frederick A.	Chapel Hill,	Prof. Fetter's.
Field, Joseph H.	Columbus, Mi.,	Miss. Mallett's.
Fleming, John M.	Wake Co.,	22, W. B.

NAME.	RESIDENCE.	ROOM.
Flythe, Augustus M.	*Northampton Co.,*	Mr. Guthrie's.
Foster, Wilbur F.	*Tuskegee, Ala.,*	Mr. Stroud's.
Foxhall, Edwin D.	*Tawborough,*	Mr. Scott's.
Frierson, Lucius	*Columbia, Tenn.,*	Mr. Hudson's.
Frierson, William	*Shelbyville, Tenn.,*	Mrs. Ashe's.
Gaines, James L.	*Asheville,*	Judge Battle's.
Gallaway, Thomas S.	*Rockingham Co.,*	Mrs. Lewis'.
Gatling, John T.	*Gates Co.,*	11, E. B.
Gill, Benjamin L.	*Franklin Co.,*	Mrs. Williams'.
Granbery, Joseph L.	*Macon, Tenn.,*	2, D. H.
Green, Berryman	*Danville, Va.,*	Mr. Nunn's.
Green, James C.	*Danville, Va.,*	Mr. Nunn's.
Green, John S.	*Memphis, Tenn.,*	Mr. Carr's.
Hamlin, Richard F.	*Calloway, Ky.,*	Mr. Weaver's.
Hampton, Manoah B.	*Lawrence Co., Ala.,*	Mr. Paxton's.
Harris, Thomas W.	*Chatham Co.,*	Miss Yancey's.
Hill, Thomas S.	*Wilmington,*	Mrs. Ashe's.
Huggins, Cooper	*Onslow Co.,*	Mr. Weaver's.
Hughes, N. Collin	*New Berne,*	21, S. B.
Isler, Simmons H.	*Goldsborough*	Mr. Watson's.
Jarratt, Thomas W.	*Montgomery Co., Ala.,*	Mr. Paxton's.
Johnston, G. Burgwin	*Edenton,*	Mr. Hunt's.
Johnston, Stuart L.	*Plymouth,*	Mr. Hunt's.
Jones, George D.	*Matagorda, Texas,*	Mr. Mickle's.
Kirkland, Alexander,	*Chapel Hill,*	Mrs. Kirkland's.
Knapp, Edwin	*Savannah, Ga.,*	Mr. Hunt's.
Knox, Andrew E. B.	*New Orleans, La.,*	Mr. Hunt's.
Kolb, Reuben F.	*Eufaula, Ala.,*	Miss. Hillyard's.
Koonce, Francis D.	*Onslow Co.,*	Mr. Guthrie's.
Latham, Louis C.	*Plymouth,*	Mr. Carr's.
Lea, Henry C.	*Mobile, Ala.,*	Mr. Guthrie's.
Lesesne, Charles	*Bladen Co.,*	Dr. Mallett's.
Lewis, Christopher C.	*Chapel Hill,*	Mrs. Lewis'.
Lewis, Richard F.	*Bladen Co.,*	Mr. Guthrie's.
Lindsay, Andrew D.	*Greensborough,*	Mr. Guthrie's.
Long, Frank P.	*Jackson, Tenn.,*	Mr. Nunn's.

NAME.	RESIDENCE.	ROOM.
Lynch, James D.	Mecklenburg Co., Va.,	Mr. Watson's.
Lynch, John B.	Mecklenburg Co., Va.;	Mr. Watson's.
Lynch, William B.	Orange Co.,	Mr. Mickle's.
McClammy, Charles W. Jr.	New Hanover Co.,	Mrs. Williams'.
McConnaughey, George C.	Rowan Co.,	Mr. Carr's.
McDonald, William	Moore Co.,	Miss Yancey's.
McEachan, Daniel P.	Robeson Co.,	Mr. Guthrie's.
McEachern, Robert J.	Robeson Co.,	21, E. B.
McQueen, James D.	Lumberton,	Mrs. Mason's.
Means, Robert A.	Columbus, Mi.,	Mr. Loader's.
Mebane, William G.	Fayette Co., Tenn.;	Mr. Nunn's.
Morrow, Calvin N.	Alamance Co.,	Mr. Stroud's.
Morrow, E. Theodore	Chapel Hill,	Mrs. Morrow's.
Murphy, Charles B.	Cumberland Co.,	Mr. Guthrie's.
Nixon, Richard W.	New Hanover Co.,	Mrs. Williams'.
Parker, Walter C. Y.	Hertford Co.,	Mr. Couch's.
Perkins, James B.	Columbus, Mi.,	Mr. Loader's.
Pillow, George M.	Columbia, Tenn.,	Mr. Nunn's.
Pinnix, Marshall H.	Caswell Co.,	6 W. B.
Purcell, John G.	Robeson Co.,	Mr. Guthrie's.
Richardson, William H.	Pickens Co., Ala.,	Mrs. Lewis'.
Richmond, Stephen D.	Milton,	Mr. Guthrie's.
Riddick, Edward L.	Gates Co.,	4, E. B.
Riddick, William T.	Gates Co.,	Mr. Couch's.
Robbins, Franklin C.	Randolph Co.,	Mr. Stroud's.
Robbins, James L.	Randolph Co.,	Mr. Stroud's.
Roberts, Isaac	Carbonton,	Mr. Weaver's.
Rogers, William J.	Northampton Co.,	Mr. Scott's.
Rugeley, Henry L.	Matagorda Co., Texas,	Mr. Marcom's.
Russ, Simpson	Bladen Co.,	Mr. Waitt's.
Saunders, Henry W.	Brunswick Co.,	Mr. Hudson's.
Satterfield, Edward F.	Roxboro,	Mr. Guthrie's.
Shannon, Nicholas B.	Okolona, Mi.,	7, E. B.
Shepard, George E.	New Hanover Co.,	Mrs. Williams'.
Shepard Joseph C.	New Hanover Co.,	Mrs. Williams'.
Sillers, William W.	Clinton,	Mr. Waitt's.

NAME.	RESIDENCE.	ROOM.
Sloan, John A.	*Greensborough,*	Mr. Thompson's.
Smith, Sydney	*Tullahatchee Co., Mi.,*	Mr. Nunn's.
Somervell, John	*Tipton Co., Tenn.,*	15, E. B.
Somervell, William J.	*Haywood Co., Tenn.,*	Mr. Thompson's.
Stockton, Francis D.	*Statesville,*	Mrs. Hargrave's.
Taylor, James P.	*Pittsborough,*	22, W. B.
Thompson, Wells	*Matagorda, Texas,*	Mr. Mickle's.
Troup, Matthew M.	*Monroe, Mi.,*	17, W. B.
Walton, Timothy	*Dayton, Ala.,*	Mr. Nunn's.
Watson, Thomas L.	*Chapel Hill,*	Mr. Watson's.
Webb, Richard S.	*Alamance Co.,*	Mr. Stroud's.
Whitfield, James G.	*Lenoir Co.,*	Mrs. Snipes'.
Wilcox, John	*Greysville, Ky.,*	Mr. Weaver's.
Williams, Joseph A.	*Pitt Co.,*	Mr. Barbee's.
Withers, Elijah B.	*Caswell Co.,*	10, W. B.
Woodburn, John A.	*Guilford Co.,*	Mr. Stroud's.

SOPHOMORE CLASS.

NAME.	RESIDENCE.	ROOM.
Adams, Robert B.	*Yorkville, S. C.,*	Mr. Hogan's.
Alexander, Sydenham B.	*Charlotte,*	18, W. B.
Allen, William T.	*Granville Co.,*	Mr. Davies'.
Anderson, Lawrence M.	*Tallahassee, Fla.,*	Mr. Nunn's.
Askew, George W.	*Columbus, Mi.,*	20, W. B.
Attmore, Isaac T.	*New Berne,*	19, S. B.
Baird, William W.	*Person Co.,*	Mr. Hogan's.
Barbee, Algernon S.	*Chapel Hill,*	Mr. Barbee's.
Barrett, Alexander	*Carthage,*	Miss Yancey's.
Barry, John D.	*Wilmington,*	16, S. B.
Battle, Junius C.	*Chapel Hill,*	Judge Battle's.
Bond, Lewis	*Brownsville, Tenn.,*	4, D. H.
Borden, William H.	*Goldsborough,*	Mr. Weaver's.
Brickell, Sterling H.	*Halifax Co.,*	Mrs. Mason's.
Brooks, William M.	*Chatham Co.,*	Mr. Weaver's.
Brown, John M.	*Iberville Par., La.,*	Mr. Carr's.
Bruce, Charles	*Halifax Co., Va.,*	Miss Hillyard's.
Bryan, George P.	*Raleigh,*	13, S. B.
Bullock, Alfred	*Williamsborough,*	Mr. Hogan's.
Bullock, Richard A.	*Williamsborough,*	Mr. Hogan's.
Butler, Lewis P.	*Tulip, Ark.,*	Mrs. Williams'.
Butler, Pierce M.	*Edgefield, S. C.,*	16, W. B.
Cates, II. P.	*Shreveport, La.,*	Mr. Guthrie's.
Cherry, William A.	*Greenville,*	24, S. B.
Cole, Alexander T.	*Richmond Co.,*	Mrs. Ashe's.
Coleman, Daniel R.	*Concord,*	2, W. B.
Cooper, Thomas W.	*Bertie Co.,*	12, E. B.
Daniel, S. Venable	*Granville Co.,*	Mr. Hogan's.
Davis, Samuel C.	*Yadkin Co.,*	12, W. B.
Davis, Thomas	*Franklin Co.,*	Mr. Waitt's.
Davis, Thomas W.	*Louisburg,*	15, S. B.

*2

NAME.	RESIDENCE.	ROOM.
DeRosset, Louis H.	*Wilmington,*	Mr. Ashe's.
Drake, Edwin L.	*Fayetteville, Tenn.,*	23, W. B.
Fain, John H. D.	*Warren Co.,*	24, E. B.
Ferrand, Horace	*Caldwell Par., La.,*	Mr. Watson's.
Fogle, James O. A.	*Columbus, Ga.,*	Mr. Davies'.
Fuller, Jesse W.	*Fayetteville,*	Mr. Carr's.
Garrett, Woodson L.	*Greene Co., Ala.,*	Mrs. Hargrave's.
Gay, Charles E.	*Columbus, Mi.,*	20, W. B.
Graham, James A.	*Hillsborough,*	6, W. B.
Graham, William	*Hillsborough,*	11, W. B.
Haigh, Charles	*Fayetteville,*	14, E. B.
Hale, Edward J. Jr.	*Fayetteville,*	Dr. Mallett's.
Headen, William J.	*Chatham Co.,*	Mr. Weaver's.
Henry, William W.	*Clarke Co., Mi.,*	Mr. Loader's.
Hicks, John H.	*Sampson Co.,*	19, E. B.
Hightower, Samuel A.	*Homer, La.,*	Mr. Hunt's.
Hogan, Henry J.	*Chapel Hill,*	Mr. Hogan's.
Holland, William A.	*Kinston,*	4, S. B.
Holt, William E.	*Alamance Co.,*	11, W. B.
Howell, R. Philip	*Goldsborough,*	6, S. B.
Jetton, Anderson C.	*Murfreesborough, Tenn.,*	Mrs. Mason's.
Jones, Edmund L.	*Rowan Co.,*	Mrs. Ashe's.
Jones, H. Francis	*Thomas Co., Ga.,*	Mr. Hogan's.
Jones, Walter J.	*Milton,*	Mr. Guthrie's.
Kelly, James	*Moore Co.,*	Mr. Weaver's.
Kelly, John B.	*Carthage,*	Mr. Weaver's.
King, William J.	*Louisburg,*	Mr. Loader's.
Lindsay, J. Harper	*Greensborough,*	21, W. B.
Little, Julius A.	*Wadesborough,*	Mr. Guthrie's.
Lutterloh, Jarvis B.	*Fayetteville,*	Dr. Mallett's.
Maclin, John W.	*Haywood Co., Tenn.,*	Mrs. Ashe's.
Martin, Eugene S.	*Wilmington,*	16, S. B.
Martin, George S.	*Maury Co., Tenn.,*	Mr. Nunn's.
McAlpine, William A.	*Eutaw, Ala.,*	Mrs. Snipes'.
McBryde, Thomas K.	*Robeson Co.,*	21, E. B.
McCallum, James B.	*Robeson Co.,*	Mrs. Mason's.

NAME.	RESIDENCE.	ROOM.
McCaskill, Neill E.	Carthage,	Miss Yancey's.
McClelland, James C.	Iredell Co.,	Mr. Loader's.
McIntyre, Kenneth M.	Moore Co.,	Mr. Weaver's.
McKellar, William H.	Dallas Co., Ala.,	Mr. Davies'.
McKethan, Edwin T.	Fayetteville,	Mr. Carr's.
McKimmon, Arthur N.	Raleigh,	17, E. B.
McKimmon, James Jr.	Raleigh,	17, E. B.
Mebane, Cornelius	Orange Co.	11, W. B.
Mebane, John W.	Fayette Co., Tenn.,	Mr. Nunn's.
Micou, Augustin	New Orleans, La.,	9, W. B.
Moore, Benjamin F.	Wadesborough,	Mr. Mickle's.
Nicholson, Robert P.	Montgomery Co.,	Mr. Davies'.
Nicholson, William T.	Halifax Co.,	Mrs. Mason's.
Nixon, Thomas F.	Wilmington,	13, S. B.
Oglesby, William M.	Sardis, Mi.,	Mr. Stroud's.
Pearce, Oliver W.	Fayetteville,	1, E. B.
Pickett, James F.	Pike Co., Ala.,	1, S. B.
Pittman, Reddin G.	Halifax Co.,	24, S. B.
Plummer, William T.	Warrenton,	Judge Battle's.
Pool, Charles C.	Elizabeth City,	Mrs. Kirkland's.
Rial, Tims	Caldwell Par., La.,	1, E. B.
Royster, Iowa M.	Raleigh,	10, E. B.
Sanders, Edward B.	Onslow Co.,	2, E. B.
Saunders, Jos. H.	Chapel Hill,	Mrs. Saunders'.
Scales, Erasmus D.	Rockingham Co.,	9, W. B.
Settle, David A.	Rockingham Co.,	2, W. B.
Sims, G. Gordon	Woodville, Mi.,	Mr. Hunt's.
Smith, Farquhard Jr.	Harnett Co.,	Mr. Loader's.
Smith, Norfleet	Halifax Co.,	5, S. B.
Smith, Thomas L.	Newport, Tenn.,	Mrs. Hargrave's.
Sterling, Edward G.	Greensborough,	Mrs. Hargrave's.
Strong, Hugh	Chester Dist., S. C.	Mr. Guthrie's.
Sykes, Richard L.	Columbus, Mi.,	Mr. Hudson's.
Taylor, George W.	Homer, La.,	Mr. Hunt's.
Taylor, James H.	Granville Co.,	3, S. B.
Thigpen, Andrew M.	Edgecombe Co.,	Mrs. Jeffrey's.

NAME.	RESIDENCE.	ROOM.
Thigpen, William A.	*Edgecombe Co.,*	Mrs. Jeffrey's.
Thorp, John H.	*Nash Co.,*	Mr. Hutchins'.
Thorp, Peterson,	*Granville Co.,*	21, W. B.
Tillery, John R.	*Halifax Co.,*	Mrs. Mason's.
Vaughan, Vernon H.	*Montgomery Co., Ala.,*	Mr. Paxton's.
Wall, James M.	*Fayette Co., Tenn.,*	Mr. Carr's.
Wallace, James A.	*Pitt Co.,*	15, E. B.
Walsh, Charles Jr.	*Mobile, Ala.,*	Mrs. Ashe's.
Weir, Samuel P.	*Greensborough,*	Mrs. Hargrave's.
West, Louis	*Woodville, Mi.,*	Mr. Hunt's.
Whitfield, Cicero	*Lenoir Co.,*	Mrs. Williams'.
Wilson, George L.	*New Berne,*	19, S. B.
Wooster, William A.	*Wilmington,*	Mr. Ashe's.

FRESHMAN CLASS.

NAME.	RESIDENCE.	ROOM.
Allen, Thomas T.	*Windsor,*	Mrs. Yancey's.
Anderson, James L.	*Winton,*	Mr. Guthrie's.
Austin, William H.	*Tawborough,*	9, E. B.
Bacot, Tours L.	*Darlington Dist., S. C.,*	32, S. B.
Ballard, Robert E.	*Louisburg,*	Mr. Carr's.
Barnes, Calvin	*Wilson,*	Mrs. Yancey's.
Barron, Charles H.	*Edgecombe Co.,*	Mr. Loader's.
Bellamy, Joseph C.	*Edgecombe Co.,*	Mrs. Yancey's.
Bond, William R.	*Halifax Co.,*	Mrs. Mason's.
Bradford, John	*Bradford, Ala.,*	Mrs. Hargrave's.
Bragg, John	*Raleigh,*	20, E. B.
Brodie, Edmund	*Granville Co.,*	Mrs. Williams'.
Bullock, George B.	*Warren Co.,*	3, S. B.
Butts, James E.	*Columbus, Ga.,*	Mr. Nunn's.
Carr, Matthew H.,	*Lenoir Co.,*	Mr. Nunn's.
Carr, William G.	*Chapel Hill,*	Mr. Carr's.
Claiborne, Felix G.	*Danville, Va.,*	Mr. Nunn's.
Clark, Pleasant B.	*Harrison Co., Texas,*	4, E. B.
Clark, Robert S.	*Upshur Co., Texas,*	4, E. B.
Coffin, R. Lawrence	*Pontotoc, Mi.,*	Mr. Watson's.
Conrad, John C.	*Yadkin Co.,*	12, W. B.
Cowan, Thomas	*Wilmington,*	16, S. B.
Craig, William H.	*Chapel Hill,*	Mr. Craig's.
Dowd, C. Furman	*Wake Co.,*	7, W. B.
Dunn, William A.	*Wake Co.,*	Mrs. Mason's.
Edmondson, Andrew K.	*Fayetteville, Tenn.,*	23, W. B.
Ely, John R.	*Marianna, Fla.,*	14, W. B.
Farabee, Benjamin F.	*Shelby Co., Tenn.,*	Mrs. Hargrave's.
Ferebee, James W.	*Princess Ann Co., Va.,*	Mr. Carr's.
Flanner, Bennet Jr.	*Wilmington,*	32, S. B.
Flowers, Oliver B.	*Warren Co., Mi.,*	Mr. Guthrie's.

NAME.	RESIDENCE.	ROOM.
Foy, David H.	New Hanover Co.,	Mr. Carr's.
Gregory, Francis R.	Granville Co.,	19, W. B.
Halliburton, John W.	Woodville, Tenn.,	1, D. H.
Harris, John W.	Chatham Co.,	Miss Yancey's.
Harris, Robert B. P.	Warren Co., Mi.,	3, E. B.
Haughton, John L.	Chatham Co.,	14, W. B.
Haughton, Thomas H.	Pittsborough,	14, W. B.
Haywood, Fabius J.	Raleigh,	18, E. B.
Hicks, John M.	Duplin Co.,	13, E. B.
Hobson, James M.	Davie Co.,	Miss Yancey's.
Hunt, James M. B.	Granville Co.,	24, W. B.
Jarratt, Isaac A.	Yadkin Co.,	12, W. B.
Jenkins, Joseph V.	Edgecombe Co.,	Mr. Loader's.
Jollee, William B.	Chapel Hill,	Mr. Jollee's.
Jones, John T.	Caldwell Co.,	Dr. Cave's.
Kenan, James G.	Kenansville,	19, E. B.
Land, John M.	Grenada, Mi.,	7, E. B.
Lane, Carma	Chatham Co.,	Mr. McDade's.
Leach, George T.	Pittsborough,	5, W. B.
Lee, Algernon M.	Clinton,	11, S. B.
Luttrell, James C. Jr.	Knoxville, Tenn.,	Judge Battle's.
Marshall, James C.	Wadesborough,	Mr. Guthrie's.
McMillan, George W.	New Hanover Co.,	Mrs. Williams'.
McSween, Murdock J.	Richmond Co.,	Mrs. Mason's.
Miller, Richard E.	Duplin Co.,	13, E. B.
Morehead, J. Turner	Greensborough,	Dr. Cave's.
Morehead, Joseph M.	Greensborough,	Miss Yancey's.
Moye, Francis M.	Stantonsburg,	Mr. Nunn's.
Murphy, Robert	Bedford Co., Tenn.,	11, S. B.
Murphy, Robert T.	Sampson Co.,	11, S. B.
Murphy, Smith	Greenwood, Mi.,	Mr. Guthrie's.
Nicholson, Guilford	Halifax Co.,	Mrs. Mason's.
Nixon, Robert J.	New Hanover Co.,	Mrs. Williams'.
Parker, James	Gates Co.,	11, E. B.
Parker, James P.	Haywood Co., Tenn.	1, D. H.
Pearson, John W.	Brandon, Mi.,	21, E. B.

NAME.	RESIDENCE.	ROOM.
Poteat, John M.	Caswell Co.,	Mr. Guthrie's.
Pugh, Robert L.	Assumption Par., La.,	Mrs. Lewis'.
Puryear, Henry S.	Huntsville,	16, W. B.
Repiton, A. Paul Jr.	Wilmington,	Mr. Ashe's.
Roan, Preston	Yanceyville,	Mr. Guthrie's.
Rhodes, William	Moore Co.,	24, E. B.
Simmons, David W. Jr.	Onslow Co.,	Mr. Carr's.
Smith David P.	DeKalb Co., Ga.,	2, P. H.
Stedman, Charles M.	Fayetteville,	Miss Hillyard's.
Taylor, Massilon F.	Granville Co.,	24, W. B.
Thompson, Charles A.	Robeson Co.,	Mrs. Mason's.
Thompson, James N.	Leasburg,	Mr. Guthrie's.
Thompson, John C.	Alamance Co.,	Mr. McDade's.
Thompson, Thomas C.	Wharton Co., Texas,	22, E. B.
Van Wyck, William Jr.	Pendleton, S. C.,	7, W. B.
Walker, Joel P.	Lauderdale Springs, Mi.,	21, E. B.
Ware, John	Brownsville, Tenn.,	4, D. H.
Whitaker, Spier Jr.	Davenport, Iowa,	2, S. B.
Whitfield, Nathan B.	Wayne Co.,	4, W. B.
Whitted, John McK.	Bladen Co.,	22, E. B.
Williams, Henry G.	Warren Co.,	Mrs. Lewis'.
Williams, Nicholas L. Jr.	Yadkin Co.,	1, W. B.
Wilson, John W.	Guilford Co.,	Mr. Craig's.
Wormely, John R.	Claiborne, Ala.,	Mr. Guthrie's.
Wright, Elisha E.	Memphis, Tenn.,	Mr. Watson's.
Wright, Joshua G. Jr.	Wilmington,	Mr. Ashe's.
Yancey, Garland M.	Chapel Hill,	Mrs. Yancey's.

PARTIAL COURSE STUDENTS.

NAME.	RESIDENCE.	ROOM.
Burgwyn, Henry K. Jr.	*Northampton Co.,*	Mrs. Snipes'.
Butts, Willis B.	*Columbus, Ga.,*	Mr. Nunn's.
Conner, Henry	*Bladen Springs, Ala.,*	24, E. B.
Cooper, Robert E.	*Sumter Dist., S. C.,*	Mr. Loader's.
Cross, William W.	*Thibodeaux, La.,*	Mrs. Lewis'.
Doxey, Samuel	*Sumner Co., Tenn.,*	Mr. Thompson's.
Goza, George W.	*Carroll Par., La.,*	Prof. Wheat's.
Hemken, Bernard B.	*Monroe, La.,*	Mrs. Ashe's.
Jernigan, John H.	*Hertford Co.,*	16, E. B.
Lassiter, Thomas	*Lenoir Co.,*	Mr. Barbee's.
Lawrence, Thomas R.	*Bertie Co.,*	Mr. Ashe's.
Lester, Robert E.	*Leon Co., Fla.,*	Mrs. Mason's.
Martin, Robert C. Jr.	*Assumption Par., La.,*	Mr. Carr's.
Martin, William W.	*Assumption Par., La.,*	Mr. Carr's.
McClure, William K.	*Arkadelphia, Ark.,*	Mr. Guthrie's.
Morrow, Edward G.	*Minden, La.,*	Mr. Weaver's.
Neal, Nathan P.	*Franklin Co.,*	Mrs. Mason's.
Pearce, Lucius R. A.	*Canton, Mi.,*	Mr. Utley's.
Pearson, William G. B.	*Bladen Co.,*	Dr. Mallett's.
Pegram, Henry B.	*New Orleans, La.,*	Mr. Carr's.
Prudhomme, Mitchell S.	*St. Landry Par., La.*	Mrs. Lewis'.
Quarles, George M.	*Minden, La.,*	Mr. Weaver's.
Satterthwaite, Lewis E.	*Pitt Co.,*	26, S. B.
Sharp, William	*Hertford Co.,*	Mr. Ashe's.
Sims, Robert N.	*Assumption Par., La.,*	Mr. Carr's.
Sims, William	*Assumption Par., La.,*	Mr. Carr's.
Tomlinson, James E.	*Johnston Co.,*	2, E. B.
Tucker, John C.	*LaFourche Par., La.,*	Mr. Guthrie's.
Whitaker, David	*Davenport, Iowa,*	2, S. B.
Williams, William S.	*Charlotte,*	22, W. B.

SUMMARY.

UNDERGRADUATES:

SENIORS,	94
JUNIORS,	119
SOPHOMORES,	116
FRESHMEN,	94
PARTIAL COURSE,	30

453

LAW STUDENTS:

INDEPENDENT CLASS,	8
COLLEGE CLASS,	20

8

SCIENTIFIC STUDENTS, - - - - - 86

Total,   461

RECAPITULATION.

NORTH CAROLINA,	293	TEXAS,	9
TENNESSEE,	35	SOUTH CAROLINA,	8
MISSISSIPPI,	28	FLORIDA,	5
LOUISIANA,	26	ARKANSAS,	3
ALABAMA,	22	IOWA,	3
GEORGIA,	10	KENTUCKY,	2
VIRGINIA,	10	NEW YORK,	1

MATRICULATES AND GRADUATES.

THE subjoined Table exhibits the number of Graduates at each Commencement since the establishment of the Institution, and (with the exceptions stated below,) the number of Matriculates during each year since the organization of the Faculty by the appointment of the late DR. CALDWELL, as President, 11th July 1804.

The first printed Catalogue of the Students appeared in 1819. It having been issued in the early part of the collegiate year, the number of Matriculates in that year, as for some time afterwards, was greater than is stated in the Table. The later Catalogues have generally contained the names of all who were connected with the Institution each year.

TABLE.

YEAR.	MATRICULATES.	GRADUATES.	YEAR.	MATRICULATES.	GRADUATES.
1798	00	7	1828	85	21
1799	00	9	1829	81	14
1800	00	3	1830	83	14
1801	00	9	1831	107	15
1802	00	3	1832	104	23
1803	00	3	1833	109	13
1804	60	6	1834	101	13
1805	57	3	1835	104	19
1806	67	4	1836	89	16
1807	40	6	1837	142	9
1808	46	13	1838	164	19
1809	37	10	1839	160	13
1810	61	3	1840	169	31
1811	54	1	1841	167	43
1812	57	10	1842	171	29
1813	97	14	1843	155	33
1814	80	16	1844	145	40
1815	88	18	1845	156	33
1816	92	15	1846	155	29
1817	108	10	1847	155	33
1818	120	14	1848	150	29
1819	110	11	1849	179	36
1820	127	25	1850	230	23
1821	146	30	1851	251	34
1822	165	28	1852	270	39
1823	173	27	1853	281	57
1824	157	34	1854	312	60
1825	122	39	1855	366	54
1826	112	19	1856	431	47
1827	76	32	1857	453	69

REQUISITES FOR ADMISSION

INTO THE

ACADEMICAL AND UNDER-GRADUATE DEPARTMENTS OF THE UNIVERSITY.

APPLICANTS for admission into the FRESHMAN CLASS are required to sustain an approved examination on the Grammars of the English, Greek, and Latin Languages; Latin Prosody; Andrews' or Arnold's Exercises; Cæsar's Commentaries; Ovid's Metamorphoses; Virgil's Bucolics, and six Books of his Æneid; Sallust; St. John's Gospel, and the Acts in the Greek Testament; Græca Minora, or Greek Reader; Arithmetic; Algebra, through equations of the first degree; Ancient and Modern Geography.

Applicants for a more advanced standing will be examined on all the studies already pursued by the class they wish to join.

The Instructors in the Greek, Latin, and Mathematical Departments have to complain that the applicants for admission are too often deficient in some part of their preparatory studies. There seems to be a disposition abroad to diminish the very limited amount of reading that is now required in Greek and Latin. There is also a lack of due preparation in the Grammars, Prosody, and construction of these languages, in Grecian and Roman Antiquities, and especially in Ancient and Modern Geography. In the Mathematics more time and practice should be devoted to problems wherein the various rules of Arithmetic are involved with more or less complexity. Unless these suggestions are regarded, Students will be unable to secure the peculiar advantages of an education at the University. For the Instructors, instead of adopting such exercises as will mature the taste and scholarship of their pupils, will be obliged to return to the drilling of the grammar school without its advantages for ensuring success.

To the teachers who are laboring to promote Classical and Mathematical learning by thorough elementary instruction we are already much indebted. We trust that our obligations to them will be still further increased; for on their efforts we must in a great measure depend for success in elevating the standard of scholarship at the University.

COURSE OF INSTRUCTION.

FRESHMAN CLASS.

FIRST TERM.	SECOND TERM.
Xenophon ; Curtius ;	Herodotus ; Virgil ; Cicero ;
Grecian History ;	Roman History ;
Algebra ; Science of Form.	Algebra ; Geometry.

SOPHOMORE CLASS.

FIRST TERM.	SECOND TERM.
Homer ; Demosthenes ;	Thucydides ; Horace ;
Horace ; French ;	Cicero ; French ;
English Composition ;	English Composition ;
Trigonometry, Surveying, &c.	Anal. Geometry ; Calculus.

JUNIOR CLASS.

FIRST TERM.	SECOND TERM.
Greek Tragedy ;	Greek Tragedy ;
Juvenal ; French ;	Cicero ; French ;
English Composition ;	English Composition ;
History, Ancient and of Middle Ages ;	Modern History ;
Chemistry and Mineralogy ;	Chemistry and Mineralogy ;
Natural Philosophy.	Astronomy.

SENIOR CLASS.

FIRST TERM.	SECOND TERM.
Mental and Moral Philosophy ;	Rhetoric ;
Political Economy ; Logic ;	Chemistry and Geology ;
Chemistry and Geology ;	International and Constitutional Law
Cicero, and Plato's Gorgias,	with Cicero, and Plato's Gorgias,
Or, the German Language ;	Or with Schiller and Goethe,
Or Studies in the Scientific School.	Or Studies in the Scientific School.

All the classes are required to attend Divine Worship in the College Chapel on Sunday forenoon, and in the afternoon to recite on the Historical parts of the Old and New Testaments.

DEPARTMENT OF GREEK.

MANUEL FETTER, A. M., Professor.
RICHARD H. BATTLE, Jr., A. M., Tutor.
SAMUEL S. JACKSON, A. M., Tutor.

The Senior Class has one recitation a week throughout the year :— the Junior Class two : and the Sophomore and Freshman Classes four each.

The Senior Class reads the Gorgias of Plato.

The Junior Class directs its attention to the Tragedies of Sophocles.

The Sophomore Class during the first term is occupied with the Iliad of Homer and select Orations of Demosthenes, and during the second with the History of the Peloponesian War by Thucydides.

The Freshman Class, in the first term, is employed upon the Anabasis of Xenophon, and in the second upon Herodotus.

DEPARTMENT OF LATIN.

REV. FORDYCE M. HUBBARD, A. M., Professor.
JOSEPH B. LUCAS, A. M., Tutor.
PETER E. SPRUILL, A. B., Tutor.
WILLIAM L. ALEXANDER, A. B., Tutor.

The Freshman and Sophomore Classes have each four recitations, the Juniors two, and the Seniors one, each week, through the year.

In the Freshman Class, the first term is spent in reading Curtius ; the second is devoted to Virgil's Georgics and Cicero's Orations. The Sophomore Class reads in the first term the Odes and Satires of Horace, and in the second the Epistles of Horace and Cicero on the Immortality of the Soul. The JUNIOR CLASS is employed during the first term upon the Satires of Juvenal, and during the second upon Cicero's Brutus. The recitations of the SENIOR CLASS are devoted to Cicero de Officiis.

DEPARTMENT OF MODERN LANGUAGES.

HILDRETH H. SMITH, A. M., PROFESSOR.

THE SOPHOMORE and JUNIOR CLASSES have each two recitations a week in French, and the SENIORS two in German throughout the year. Volunteer classes are taught Spanish and Italian in the SENIOR year.

SOPHOMORE CLASS.

Ollendorff's French Grammar; Arnoult's French Reader; and Selection's from Molière's Comedies.

JUNIOR CLASS.

Racine's Tragedies; Dumas' History of Napoleon, and Rowan's Modern French Reader.

SENIOR CLASS.

FIRST TERM.   Ollendorff's German and Spanish Grammars;
               Adler's German Reader, and Don Quixote.
SECOND TERM.   Schiller's Maid of Orleans; Goethe's Iphigenia
               in Tauris; Monti's Italian Grammar, and Tasso's Jerusalem Delivered.

DEPARTMENT OF HISTORY.

REV ALBERT M. SHIPP, A. M., PROFESSOR.

THE FRESHMAN and JUNIOR CLASSES have each two recitations a week, throughout their respective years.

The FRESHMAN CLASS is occupied with the History of Greece in the first term, and in the second with Roman History. The JUNIOR CLASS in the first term completes the study of Ancient History together with the History of the Middle Ages. The second term is devoted exclusively to Modern History—special attention being given to that of England and America

Throughout the entire course, the classes will be guided to the best sources of information on all the more important subjects of Historical inquiry, and stimulated to extend their investigations beyond the text books, by making a free use of the collateral aids supplied by the Libraries of the University and of the two Literary Societies. The text books recommended in this Department are Smith's History of Greece, Liddell's Rome, Smith's Gibbon, and Smyth's Lectures on Modern History.

DEPARTMENT OF LOGIC AND RHETORIC.

REV. JOHN T. WHEAT, D. D., PROFESSOR.

INSTRUCTION in this Department is first given to the SOPHOMORE CLASS. It is required to write Compositions every third week; and as the benefit proposed does not consist in the intrinsic value of the composition, but in the *exercise* to the writer's mind, care is taken to select such subjects as will afford that exercise. Particular attention is also paid to spelling, punctuation, the precise meaning of words, good taste in the forms of expression, and the various particulars of a correct "proof reading."

In the second term, lectures are given upon the origin and growth of the English Language; chiefly with a view to purity and precision of style in regard to its idioms and anomalies.

In the JUNIOR year the topics are :—Habits of reading and writing for the proper conduct of the Understanding : Forms and Tribunals of Taste and Criticism : Elocution and the different kinds of Oratory.—The Class has also occasional exercises in extemporaneous speaking and debate.

The SENIOR CLASS has two recitations a week in Whately's Logic and Rhetoric ; and, at the close of the second term, each one is required to pronounce, in public, an Oration of his own composition.

D.EPARTMENT OF MATHEMATICS.

REV. JAMES PHILLIPS, D. D., Professor.
CHARLES PHILLIPS, A. M., Assistant Professor.
SOLOMON POOL, A. M., Tutor.
THADDEUS C. COLEMAN, Tutor.
JOHN W. GRAHAM, A. B., Tutor.

FRESHMAN CLASS.

First Term. Peirce's Algebra, through Equations of the second degree; Munroe's Geometry and Science of Form.

Second Term. Peirce's Algebra, through Geometrical Progression; Peirce's Geometry.

SOPHOMORE CLASS.

First Term. Phillips' Plane and Spherical Trigonometry with its applications to Navigation, Heights, Distances, Surveying, &c.

Second Term. Loomis' Differential Calculus; Loomis' Integral Calculus.

JUNIOR CLASS.

First Term. Olmsted's Natural Philosophy.
Second Term. Norton's Astronomy.

During the Freshman, Sophomore, and Junior years four recitations a week are devoted to the studies in Pure and mixed Mathematics. The Professor of Mathematics and Natural Philosophy superintends all these studies as to the text books to be used, the parts of each to be omitted, the time to be occupied by the rest, and the attainments to be required from the Students. But in the instruction of the different classes he avails himself of such aid from the Assistant Professor and the Tutors as he may require.

One of the four recitations during the Junior year is appropriated to Lectures on Natural Philosophy and Astronomy, by the Assistant

Professor. These Lectures embrace all the topics disscussed in the text books, and others more or less closely connected with them, and are fully illustrated by appropriate experiments. The Partial Course Students and pupils in the Scientific School, whose tastes and acquirements may enable them to profit by these lectures, can obtain permission to attend them by applying to the Professor.

It will be seen that the organization of an Analytical, as distinct from a Geometrical course of Mathematics, during the SOPHOMORE and JUNIOR years, has been abandoned. It was begun as an experiment in 1855; but a full trial has shown that the advantages of the plan have so far been counterbalanced by its disadvantages. Therefore our own former, and the almost universal practice in this respect by institutions of similar organization has been revived. Members of the same class and colleagues in study receive almost as much education from one another as they do from their teachers. So it has been found advisable to maintain the interest in each other's pursuits that should pervade a large body of students, and not deprive the less successful of the assistance which superior talents and better opportunities for education may enable some of their classmates to render them. Those who have time enough, and are qualified to make the researches, are constantly urged to all the investigations in Mathematics which their own curiosity, or their teachers and the libraries around them may suggest.

DEPARTMENT OF
CHEMISTRY, MINERALOGY, GEOLOGY,
WILLIAM J. MARTIN, Professor.

On these branches, four lectures, illustrated by appropriate experiments and the exhibitions of specimens, are commonly delivered, every week, to the Senior and Junior classes, two to each; which such persons pursuing a Partial Course as choose to apply themselves to these studies, have an opportunity of attending. The Lecture is succeeded, after an interval of an hour or an hour and a half, by an examination extending through one hour, upon the facts and doctrines that were its subject; and upon others, the knowledge of which may contribute to a better understanding of the Lecture that is next to follow. With these, the Student is expected to make himself acquainted, by means of notes taken at the time, a volume that is placed in his hands, or some other book of elements.

The history of Chemistry, its Nomenclature, and General Doctrines, the Imponderables, (under which head the phenomena and laws of Light, Heat, Electricity, and Galvanism, are treated of, at such length as their relations to the science of Chemistry seem to require,) and the non-metallic elements occupy the Junior year. In the Senior year, the non-metallic elements, if any part remains unfinished, are completed—with the Chemistry of the Metals, and of Organized bodies.

In Natural History, the sciences of Botany and Zoology receive attention, so far only, as is necessary to a knowledge of their methods, the classification, and the means employed for distinguishing different plants and animals from each other. A much larger portion of time is devoted during the Junior year to Mineralogy, and pains taken to render the student familiar at least with the more common and useful minerals. With reference to this object, a very sufficient collection has been made, and is increasing from year to year, of such species as the rocks of North Carolina, especially, afford, but which contains many specimens from the neighboring States, and distant parts of the world. To this the Student has free access, and ample opportunity of learning to distinguish one species from another. The Cabinet purchased some years since in Vienna affords additional facilities, where a more accurate knowledge of the Science is desired.

Geology is taught throughout the Senior year.

DEPARTMENT OF
MORAL PHILOSOPHY, METAPHYSICS,
POLITICAL ECONOMY, INTERNATIONAL
AND CONSTITUTIONAL LAW.

THE PRESIDENT.

INSTRUCTION in these branches is given the SENIOR CLASS three days (five recitations) of every week in the Collegiate year.

Metaphysics and Political Economy receive attention during the first term. The Sunday Recitations throughout the year are devoted to the Old Testament and Moral Science ; and in addition, the recitations on Monday afternoon of the second term, are ordinarily assigned to the latter study.

The text books are : The BIBLE, Wayland's Moral Science, Abercrombie's Inquiries concerning the Intellectual Powers, (Abbott's Edition); Wayland's Political Economy ; Sheppard's Constitutional Text Book ; and the first volume of Kent's Commentaries on American Law.

No portion of the text books (except the Bible, instruction in which is confined to the Pentateuch,) is omitted, but the whole is carefully recited, subsequently reviewed, and each member of the class separately and rigidly examined on the entire system.

Oral lectures are given whenever, in the opinon of the Instructor, hey are calculated to promote the improvement of the class ; and, towards the close of the second term, a regular course is delivered on the History of Constitutional Law, presenting an analytical review, in chronological order, of the Magna Charta of King John ; the Petition of Right ; the Charters of Carolina ; the Fundamental Constitutions, (by John Locke); the Habeas Corpus Act ; the Bill of Rights ; the Declaration of Independence ; the Articles of Confederation ; the Treaty of Peace with Great Britain ; and the Constitution of the United States.

SCHOOL FOR THE

APPLICATION OF SCIENCE TO THE ARTS.

HON. DAVID L. SWAIN, LL. D., PRESIDENT.

REV. JAMES PHILLIPS, D. D., PROFESSOR.

CHARLES PHILLIPS, A. M., PROFESSOR.

JOHN KIMBERLY, A. M., PROFESSOR.

WILLIAM J. MARTIN, PROFESSOR.

SCIENTIFIC STUDENTS.

NAME.	RESIDENCE.	STUDIES.
Adams, William	Greensborough,	Agr. & Anal. Chem.
Allen, Edward L.	Fayetteville, Tenn.,	Agr. & Anal. Chem.
Anderson, Robert W.	New Hanover Co.,	Engineering.
Baker, James S.	Jackson Co., Fla.,	Agr. & Anal. Chem.
Benbury, Lemuel C.	Edenton,	Agr. & Anal. Chem.
Bitting, John H.	Germanton,	Agr. & Anal. Chem.
Bonner, William Jr.	Fayetteville, Tenn.,	Agr. & Anal. Chem.
Brinson, Samuel M.	New Berne,	Agr. & Anal. Chem.
Brown, Joseph A. C.	Davidson Co.,	Engineering.
Bruce, Wilkins	Halifax Co., Va.,	Eng.; Anal. Chem.
Buchanan, John B.	Richmond Co.,	Engineering.
Burgwyn, Henry K. Jr.	Northampton Co.,	Engineering.
Clark, Nevin D. J.	Montgomery Co.,	Agr. & Anal. Chem.
Clement, Samuel W.	Granville Co.,	Agr. & Anal. Chem.
Conner, Henry	Bladen Springs, Ala.,	Engineering.
Cowan, Thomas Jr.,	Wilmington,	Agr. & Anal Chem.
Cox, Cader G.	Onslow Co.,	Agr. & Anal. Chem.
Cross, William W.	Thibodeaux, La.,	Engineering.
Davie, Ambrose Jr.	Montgomery Co., Tenn.,	Engineering.
Faison, Peter B.	Lagrange, Tenn.,	Engineering.

NAME.	RESIDENCE.	STUDIES.
Foreman, William J.	*Pitt, Co.,*	Agr. & Anal. Chem.
Gibson, John P.	*Concord,*	Agr. & Anal. Chem.
Gibson, William H.	*Concord,*	Agr. & Anal. Chem.
Gilmer, John A. Jr.	*Greensborough,*	Agr. & Anal. Chem.
Goodloe, David S. Jr.	*Madison Co., Mi.*	Agr. Chem.
Goodloe, Winter H.	*Madison Co., Mi.*	Agr. & Anal. Chem.
Goodman, John C.	*Gates Co.,*	Agr. & Anal. Chem.
Goza, S. Dupuy	*Carroll Par., La.,*	Agr. & Anal. Chem.
Groover, James I.	*Thomas Co., Ga.,*	Agr. & Anal. Chem.
Harris, Thomas B.	*Warrenton, Ala.,*	Agr. & Anal. Chem.
Harvey, Addison	*Canton, Mi.,*	Agr. Chem.
Hemken, Bernard B.	*Monroe, La.,*	Agr. & Anal. Chem.
Hilliard, Louis	*Nash Co.,*	Agr. & Anal. Chem.
Humphries, Wm. W. Jr.	*Columbus, Mi.,*	Agr. & Anal. Chem.
Hunt, James D.	*Izard Co., Ark.,*	Agr. & Anal. Chem.
Isler, Stephen W.	*Goldsborough,*	Agr. & Anal. Chem.
Johnson, Francis M.	*Davie Co.,*	Agr. & Anal. Chem.
Johnston, Robert D.	*Lincoln Co.,*	Agr. & Anal. Chem.
Johnston, Zebulon M.	*Cabarrus Co.,*	Agr. & Anal. Chem.
Jones, Hamilton C. Jr.	*Rowan Co.,*	Agr. & Anal. Chem.
Kerr, William L.	*Alamance Co.,*	Agr. & Anal. Chem.
Lassiter, Thomas	*Lenoir Co.,*	Agr. & Anal. Chem.
Little, William	*Raleigh,*	Agr. & Anal. Chem.
Macartney, Thomas N.	*Mobile, Ala.,*	Agr. & Anal. Chem.
Mann, Rufus B.	*Granville Co.,*	Agr. & Anal. Chem.
Marsh, James A.	*Asheborough,*	Agr. & Anal. Chem.
Martin, Robert C. Jr.	*Assumption Par., La.,*	Engineering.
Martin, William W.	*Assumption Par., La.,*	Engineering.
McAlister, Alexander C.	*Randolph Co.,*	Agr. Chem.
McConnaughey, Joseph L.	*Rowan Co.,*	Agr. & Anal. Chem.
Murphy, William	*Salisbury,*	Agr. & Anal. Chem.
Neal, Nathan P.	*Franklin Co.,*	Engineering.
Pearson, William G. B.	*Bladen Co.,*	Eng. ; Agr. Chem.
Perry, John M.	*Beaufort,*	Agr. Chem.
Philips, Frederick	*Edgecombe Co.,*	Agr. & Anal. Chem.
Prudhomme, Mitchell S.	*St. Landry Par., La.,*	Engineering.

NAME.	RESIDENCE.	STUDIES.
Richmond, John M.	*Fairfield Dist., S. C.,*	Agr. & Anal. Chem.
Ringo, Joseph H.	*Fayetteville, Tenn.,*	Anal. Chem.
Scales, James T.	*Henry Co., Va.,*	Agr. & Anal. Chem.
Sims, Robert N.	*Assumption Par., La.,*	Engineering.
Sims, William	*Assumption Par., La.,*	Engineering.
Singeltary, Richard W.	*Pitt Co.,*	Agr. & Anal. Chem.
Smith, Benjamin G.	*Halifax Co.,*	Agr. & Anal. Chem.
Sutton, William T. Jr.	*Bertie Co.,*	Agr. & Anal. Chem.
Swain, Richard C.	*Chapel Hill,*	Agr. & Anal. Chem.
Sykes, Edward T.	*Columbus, Mi.,*	Agr. & Anal. Chem.
Sykes, S. Turner	*Aberdeen, Mi.,*	Agr. & Anal. Chem.
Tate, Henry H.	*Gaston Co.,*	Agr. & Anal. Chem.
Tate, John W.	*Gaston Co.,*	Agr. & Anal. Chem.
Tatum, John D	*Milledgeville, Ga.,*	Engineering.
Twitty, William L.	*Rutherford Co.,*	Agr. & Anal. Chem.
Wade, Thomas B.	*Williamson Co., Tenn.,*	Agr. & Anal. Chem.
Walker, James A.	*Wilmington,*	Agr. & Anal. Chem.
Washington, Augustine B.	*Memphis, Tenn.,*	Agr. & Anal. Chem.
Watlington, James S.	*Caswell Co.,*	Agr. & Anal. Chem.
Whitaker, David	*Davenport, Iowa,*	Agr. & Anal. Chem.
Whitaker, William	*Davenport, Iowa,*	Agr. Chem.
White, Joseph M.	*Marianna, Fla.,*	Agr. & Anal. Chem.
Whitehead, Willie W.	*Kenansville,*	Eng. ; Agr. Chem.
Whitfield, Boaz	*Demopolis, Ala.,*	Agr. & Anal. Chem.
Whitted, Thomas S.	*Bladen Co.,*	Agr. & Anal. Chem.
Williams, Joseph	*Yadkin Co.,*	Agr. & Anal. Chem.
Williamson, John W.	*Caswell Co.,*	Agr. & Anal. Chem.
Young, David J.	*Granville Co.,*	Agr. & Anal. Chem.
Young, William H.	*Granville Co.,*	Agr. Chem.

The Scientific Students are candidates either for the degree of Bachelor of Arts, or for that of Bachelor of Science. The former are such members of the SENIOR CLASS as are permitted to substitute studies in this School for the Ancient Languages during their first term, or for the Ancient Languages, and International and Constitutional Law during their second term. If these Students spend a fifth year at the University they may obtain the degree of Master of Arts. The degree of Bachelor of Science may be conferred on those who devote their time chiefly to the studies prescribed in the Scientific School.— This course will generally require an attendance of two years and a half. But, as is usual, in beginning his labors any such Student will be admitted to the standing for which he is qualified by his acquisitions.

The instructions afforded in the Departments of this School are intended to prepare young men for professional life, as Artizans, Engineers, Farmers, Miners, and Physicians. The Students will have frequent opportunities for the practice of rules of their professions. But their attention will rather be directed to the obtaining of a familiar acquaintance with the theories and principles by which the Science of the day most vigorously advances the Arts of Civilization.

The Scientific Students will be subject to the general oversight and discipline of the Faculty of the University. Their attendance on Recitations, Prayers, Public Worship, &c., is expected to be as punctual and their responsibility to all the laws of the University to be as complete as is that of the Students in the Academical Departments.

DEPARTMENT OF CIVIL ENGINEERING.

CHARLES PHILLIPS, A. M., PROFESSOR.

APPLICANTS for admission into this Department will be expected to manifest great familiarity with the various processes in Arithmetic, Algebra, Geometry, and Plane and Spherical Trigonometry, together with their applications in Surveying, Navigation, Heights and Distances. These preliminary acquisitions are indispensable. At present, the studies in this department are arranged as follows:

FIRST YEAR.

Analytical Geometry; Differential and Integral Calculus ; Davies' Descriptive Geometry ; Davies' Shades and Shadows.

SECOND YEAR.

Smith's Mechanics ; Mahan's Civil Engineering ; Gillespie on Roads and Railways ; Trautwine, Borden, Long, &c., on Geodesy and Earth Works.

THIRD YEAR.

Application of Science to various constructive Arts; Reviews of previous studies.

Mechanical, Topographical, and Architectural drawing, both plain and isometrical, will be taught throughout the whole course. The theories, involved in the construction and adjustment of instruments, together with their uses in the field, and exercises in the resulting computations, will be attended to in their proper seasons. Besides the studies peculiar to this Department, its pupils will pursue such in Analytical Chemistry, and in the Academical Departments as may be necessary to the ends they have in view.

DEPARTMENT FOR THE
APPLICATION OF CHEMISTRY

TO

AGRICULTURE AND THE ARTS.

JOHN KIMBERLY, A. M., PROFESSOR.

STUDENTS in this Department will receive instructions in Analytical Chemistry, and its applications to the analysis of soils and manures the assaying of ores and minerals, the analysis of mineral waters, and the testing of drugs and medicines. An Analytical Laboratory has been fitted up in one of the buildings of the University, and will be open for Students every day in the Week, during each term, so that those who desire it may occupy all their time in performing the various operations in practical Chemistry.

Particular attention will be given to the Chemistry of Agriculture, by recitations as well as lectures, during each term of the course.

The text-books for reading and reference are: Will's Outlines of Chemical Analysis; Rose's Analytical Chemistry; Regnault's Chemistry; Stockhardt's Field Lectures; Plattner's testing with the Blowpipe, and Bowman's Medical Chemistry.

LAW SCHOOL.

HON. DAVID L. SWAIN, LL. D., PRESIDENT.
HON. WILLIAM H. BATTLE, LL. D., PROFESSOR.
SAMUEL F. PHILLIPS, A. M.

INDEPENDENT CLASS.

NAME.	RESIDENCE.	ROOM.
Anthony, John	*Halifax,*	Mr. Ashe's.
Harrell, Hiram P.	*Bertie Co.,*	Mr. Howell's.
Hayley, Leonidas N. B.	*Franklin Co., Ala,,*	Mr. Watson's.
Knapp, Edwin	*Savannah, Ga.,*	Mr. Phillips'.
McLean, William P.	*Cass Co , Texas,*	Mr. Mickle's.
McNab, James G.	*Eufaula, Ala,,*	Miss Hillyard's.
Mitchell, Lueco	*Salisbury,*	Mr. Carr's.
Ward, Nathan P.	*Franklin Co,,*	Mrs. Kirkland's.

COLLEGE CLASS.

NAME.	RESIDENCE.	ROOM.
Anderson, Robert W.	*New Hanover Co.,*	Mr. Hunt's.
Bell, Edward S.	*Bladen Springs, Ala.,*	Mr. Jollee's.
Benbury, Lemuel C.	*Edenton,*	President Swain's.
Brinson, Samuel M.	*New Berne,*	26, S. B.
Brown, Hugh T.	*Wilkesborough,*	Prof. Smith's.
Clarke, Nevin D. J.	*Montgomery Co.,*	Mr. Weaver's.
Dugger, Macon T.	*Warrenton,*	Mrs. Mason's.
Harvey, Addison	*Canton, Mi.,*	Mr. Marcom's,
Hay, Phillip T.	*Rockingham Co.,*	Mrs. Ashe's,
Hilliard, Louis	*Nash Co.,*	Miss Mallett's,
Hunt, James D.	*Izard Co., Ark.,*	Mr. Mickle's
Jernigan, John H.	*Hertford Co.,*	16, E. B.
Jones, Hamilton C. Jr.	*Rowan Co.,*	Mrs. Ashe's.
Mason, Thomas W.	*Brunswick Co., Va.,*	President Swain's.
Perry, John M.	*Beaufort,*	Mr. Mickle's.
Phillips, Frederick	*Edgecombe Co.,*	Mr. Marcom's.

NAME.	RESIDENCE.	ROOM.
Tucker, John C.	*LaFourche Par., La.,*	Mr. Guthrie's.
Whitaker, William	*Davenport, Iowa,*	23, E. B.
Whitehead, Willie W.	*Kenansville,*	Mr. Barbee's.
Whitfield, Boaz	*Demopolis, Ala.,*	Mr. Hudson's.

This Department contains two Classes, of which the first, called the Independent Class, consists of such Students of Law as have no connexion with any of the College Classes; and the second, called the College Class, of such Members of College as, with the permission of the Faculty, may be desirous of joining it.

The plan of Studies comprises Blackstone's Commentaries; Cruise's Digest of Real Property; Fearne on Remainders; Iredell on Executors; Stephen on Pleading; Chitty's Pleading; Selwyn's Nisi Prius; Smith on Contracts; Greenleaf on Evidence, and Adams' Doctrine of Equity; together with lectures on the Common Law having special reference to the Legislation and Judicial decisions of North Carolina. A complete course will occupy two years for the Independent Class, at the end of which, the degree of Bachelor of Laws is conferred on such students as, by their proficiency, may be entitled to it.

The Independent Class is called on for recitations three times a week. The recitations of the College Class occur only once a week, and are so arranged as not to interfere with the ordinary duties of College.

A Moot Court will be held occasionally by one of the Professors, for the discussion, by the Students, of such legal questions as he may propose. The Student will also be required, from time to time, to draw pleadings, and other legal instruments, and be instructed in the practice of the Courts.

The Professors of Law receive no salary from the Trustees of the University; but are entitled to demand from each member of the Independent Class fifty dollars per session for the first two sessions of the course, and twenty-five dollars per session afterwards; and from each member of the College Class twenty-five dollars per session. The sessions and vacations of this department are the same as those of the College, but the Professors will give instructions during the vacations to such members of either class as desire it, without an extra charge.

The Professors of Law, and the members of the Independent Class, are not subject to any of the ordinary College regulations.

ANNUAL EXPENSES.

TUITION	- $50.00	-	$50.00
ROOM RENT	10.00	-	- 10.00
SERVANT HIRE	- 5.00	-	5.00
DEPOSIT	6.00	-	- 600
BOARD FOR 40 WEEKS	100.00	TO	140.00
BED AND WASHING	20.00	"	24.00
WOOD,	- 5.00	"	10.00
LIGHTS	5.00	"	6.00
TOTAL	201.00	"	251.00

To the above items are to be added the expenses for clothing and pocket money, and certain others incident to a connexion with the two Literary Societies. The cost of the whole series of text-books required in the College course varies from $55 to $65.

The above statement applies to those who occupy rooms in the College buildings :—those who lodge in the Village are subjected to an additional expenditure for Room Rent and Servant Hire.

The Laws of the University require that every Student shall, at the beginning of each session, settle the TUITION, &c., in advance ; and the attention of Parents and Guardians is particularly directed to this regulation.

It is the duty of the Bursar (PROF. FETTER,) to receive on deposit the funds which a Student may bring with him, or which may be remitted to him ;—to disburse them in payment of necessary or contingent expenses, and to render an account of the same to Parents and Guardians at the close of each session.

From what has been mentioned it will be seen what amount of money is necessary for the current expenses of a year. If the regulations of the Trustees and the "Act concerning the University" are strictly complied with, Parents and Guardians may feel confident that the expenses will not exceed those enumerated above. The Faculty of the University entertains the opinion that exclusive of clothing and travelling expenses, Three Hundred and Twenty-Five Dollars per annum are amply sufficient for all necessary purposes.

The Faculty is authorized in all cases where the applicant is a native of this State, sustains a correct moral character, is believed to possess good talents and studious habits, and is unable to defray the expenses of Tuition and Room Rent, to admit him free of charge into any class for which he may be prepared.